adventure

THE
CROSSING

A
Richard Jackson
Book

ALSO BY GARY PAULSEN

Dogsong

Dancing Carl

Tracker

Sentries

Hatchet

THE
CROSSING

GARY PAULSEN

ORCHARD BOOKS·NEW YORK·LONDON
A division of Franklin Watts, Inc.

Orchard Books
387 Park Avenue South
New York, NY 10016

Orchard Books Canada
20 Torbay Road
Markham, Ontario 23P 1G6

Orchard Books is a division of Franklin Watts, Inc.

Manufactured in the United States of America
Book design by Mina Greenstein
The text of this book is set in 12 pt. Caslon 540.
2 4 6 8 10 9 7 5 3 1

Library of Congress Cataloging-in-Publication Data
Paulsen, Gary. The crossing.
Summary: Fourteen-year-old Manny, a street kid
fighting for survival in a Mexican border town, devel-
ops a strange friendship with an emotionally disturbed
American soldier who decides to help him get across
the border. [1. Mexico—Fiction. 2. Emotional
problems—Fiction] I. Title.
PZ7.P2843Cr 1987 [Fic] 87-7738
ISBN 0-531-05709-8 ISBN 0-531-08309-8 (lib. bdg.)

THIS IS FOR RAY

THE
CROSSING

THE
FIRST
MEETING

1

*M*anny *Bustos* awakened when the sun cooked the cardboard over his head and heated the box he was sleeping in until even a lizard could not have taken it, and he knew, suddenly, that it was time. This was the day. He would make the crossing today.

Juárez, Mexico, was never quiet. As a border town it was made of noise—noise that filled all the hours of the day—but the noises changed, and he listened to them now without thinking. Honking horns, the market starting to fill with people trying to get fresh goat cheese or the thick coffee, people yelling insults and curses at each other—a hum of noise. Mornings were the best time, not a good time—there were no good times for him—but the best. He lived on the street, moving, always moving because he was fourteen and had red hair and large brown eyes with long lashes, and there was danger if he did not move— danger from the men who would take him and sell him to those who wanted to buy fourteen- year-old street boys with red hair and long eyelashes.

So now he rolled out when the sun warmed the cardboard of his lean-to, wiped his mouth with a finger, and stood to begin moving for the day. Another day in Juárez. But this time it was dif- ferent. This day he would change it all; he would leave. This day he would cross to the north to the United States and find work, become a man, make money, and wear a leather belt with a large buckle and a straw hat with a feathered hatband.

Hunger was instant, had never gone. He went to bed hungry, slept hungry, awakened hungry, had hunger every moment of every day, and could not remember when he did not have hunger. Even when he was small, a baby in the back of the Church of Our Lady of Perpetual Sorrow where his unknown mother had left him in an box and the sisters had tried to feed him, there was hunger. It was almost a friend, the hunger, if something could be a friend and be hated at the same time, and he set out now to find the first food of the day.

He tucked the T-shirt into his torn pants and ran his fingers through his hair. It did almost no good—his hair was wiry and thick and full and resisted any attempts at straightening—but it was an automatic gesture, and he jammed in the loose ends when he put the baseball cap on. Across the front of the cap it said Ford.

Manny moved through the alley in back of the church and made for the back of the Two-by-Four bar and café, near the strip of Santa Fe Street where the bridge crossed over from El Paso into Juárez. Most of the bars and clubs and places with women were for the tourists and soldiers who came over from Fort Bliss and were not open yet. But the Two-by-Four was open early to catch the people who were going to the market, had been open since three o'clock.

It was a simple place to eat. In the front was a large gas grill with pipes filled with tiny holes for the gas to burn in rows of blue flames. Past this rotated a rack with whole chickens on steel rods.

On a stove to the side was a large pot of beans—frijoles—and at four booths were bowls of salsa with seeds and so hot even Manny, who had a tongue of iron, could not eat it. In the rear of the café was a large steel drum with a flame in it and a flat piece of steel on top for cooking tortillas. At the drum stood Maria—Manny thought of her always as Old Maria although she was not so old—taking the corn dough in small pieces and slapping it flat with her palms, slapping it to drop it on the hot tin, flicking it over with her fingers when it was smoking, cooking the other side until it was done and brown and adding it to a stack of tortillas that never seemed to grow because people ate them with the chicken and salsa as fast as she could cook them.

If he stood long enough and smiled in the shy way, Old Maria would sometimes hand him a tortilla and he could get some beans from the pot if he was lucky, and that would cut away the hunger for a time. Once a drunken soldier had believed his limp when it was dark and he was begging and had given him five American dollars, which none of the larger boys had seen and so he had managed to keep it. At the time he was only five or six—he did not know his true age—and five American dollars was a fortune. He had taken it to the Two-by-Four and bought a chicken and tortillas and Pepsi Cola and had eaten and eaten until nothing but bones remained.

That had been a time, that day. He had not gotten full, but there had been something close to it, and he could still close his eyes, eight years later, and remember the taste of the grease and the garlic on his face, the feeling of his stomach swollen with food and not with hunger. He had spent over half of the five dollars just on food and would have spent it all had a larger boy not seen him eating and known that he had money and taken the rest from him. Even so, with just half of it, there had been much food—a whole chicken and a stack of tortillas.

He arrived at the back of the Two-by-Four and stopped outside the screened alley door. It was hot in the alley and the garbage smells were getting strong, but still the odor of the cooking chicken and the scorching tortillas rolled through the screen and took him. His stomach rumbling, he looked through the screen to see Maria standing by the metal cooker, and he smiled the shy smile.

"Hello, beautiful lady. How is your morning?"

Maria looked through the screen and laughed. "I could set my watch by you if I had a watch. First the sun, then the heat, then Manny Bustos coming for his breakfast." She finished slapping a tortilla and threw it on the tin, flicked four of them over, then picked up some corn dough and started making a new one. Some hair had come loose from the leather tie-back and hung down the side of her face. It was rich and thick, and black but for a small streak of flour in it where she had used her hand to push it back. "I can let you have a tortilla but the frijoles aren't ready yet."

Manny nodded. "I would be very grateful for a tortilla. Your tortillas are the best I have ever eaten."

"So smooth, so smooth. You are as smooth as my first husband when he came to talk to me of the moon and beauty. . . ." She opened the screen and handed him a tortilla fresh off the stove, so hot he had to juggle it with his fingers to keep from burning them. When it was only slightly cool he rolled it expertly in a tube and ate it in two bites. One tortilla was small, and it really only served to make his appetite worse, but he held back on pushing for more. He had bigger thoughts.

"Later in this day I will be leaving," he said, lowering his voice as he thought a man would speak. "It is time for me to be crossing to the north and finding work."

She studied him through the screen. A dozen flies worked to get in, making a high buzzing sound that somehow matched the talking sounds of the café in front. "You are too young to make the crossing."

Manny shrugged. "It is not age. I am ready to make the crossing and so it is time. Age does not matter."

"But you are small."

"I am not so small." He bridled. "I have strength and I am fast and I know how to work hard. That is all that is required to cross to the north. They only wish you to work hard."

She sighed. Two tortillas started to burn and she took them off the stove, then added some more corn dough to the red-hot metal. "The coyotes will have you. They are not good people, the coyotes who take people across the border. They will have you and they will sell you."

Manny brushed the flies from the screen. "It cannot be worse than now. Every day I must watch for those who would sell me. Besides, I will not use coyotes. I will cross myself, alone. This night in the dark I will become like the night and I will cross and then I will find a ride in the back of a truck and head north. There is much work there. I will find work and make money and buy new pants and a new shirt with the silver snaps and a new belt with a large buckle and perhaps a new pair of boots. I will cross tonight and I will do all of that . . ."

Maria continued the rhythm of the slapping, the tortillas flowing in an endless stream from the dough, through her hands, onto the stove, and in to the waiting customers. "If you are so sure of all this, why do you come to tell me?"

Now he hesitated. What he wanted had to be asked for correctly and with courtesy. "I will go tonight, and there is much work to be had, but it is perhaps possible that I will not find work at once. I may have to go a day, I may have to go even two days . . ." He trailed off.

"And you want food," she finished for him. "You come to me for food."

He nodded. "If I had a chicken, one of those delicious chickens, and a few tortillas, I could go for days. It is possible that I can pay you. This afternoon I will go to the bridge and work the turistas, and there may be enough money to pay. But if not I wish to borrow a chicken and some tortillas."

"Borrow?" She snorted. "You wish to borrow a chicken?"

"Si. Yes. I will pay you later, send you money for the chicken."

And at first he thought she would say no. There was that in her mouth, he thought, the no was in her mouth. But instead her eyes took on a sadness he did not understand. It was a sadness for him, but more it seemed to be a sadness, a pity, for herself. She sighed again. "Come back this evening. I will still be working. Come to the back door just at dark and I will have a chicken in a paper sack for you. But wait until I am standing alone to knock. The owner comes in the afternoon and stays for the evening. He will not be pleased if he sees me giving you food."

Manny smiled. "I owe you much for this. Thank you. Thank you and know that I will find a way to pay."

"Don't talk of pay. You have nothing and will have nothing for the time that you live. But you cannot see that now. So cross tonight and I will feed you and maybe it will be that you are lucky, one of the lucky ones." She brushed the hair back. "And now leave. Just talking to you makes me feel old and tired."

Manny thanked her once more and moved off into the alley, headed for the bridge. It was still too early for the tourists to start flowing across it, but he had to get his money-catcher ready and perhaps fight for a place beneath the bridge.

He had much to do to get ready, and on this day he did not have much time left.

He would cross tonight.

2

*H*e *was*, above all things, a sergeant.

Robert S. Locke looked in the full-length mirror on the door of his barracks room—above the mirror was a sign in large block letters: A SOLDIER IS ALWAYS NEAT, CHECK YOUR APPEARANCE DAILY—and studied himself carefully. He thought, even now, even with the slippage from the Cutty Sark Scotch whiskey and the clouded vision that was coming as the whiskey took him, even with all that he was still, above all things, a sergeant.

The man in the mirror didn't look like he felt.

The man in the mirror was ramrod straight with graying, short, tight hair and a straight mouth. The man in the mirror had an in-line nose, even steel-blue eyes with just a faint shade of red in the whites now, a shave so close the skin looked raw, flat ears, and a uniform so incredibly neat and sharp and true that the cloth looked to be carved from stone; a granite uniform. Even the rows of decorations seemed carved against his barrel chest.

The man in the mirror showed only one scar, the one from the tiny bit of shrapnel in Vietnam that had cut white-sizzling across his left temple and missed ending him by less than a quarter inch. The reflection showed none of the true scars— the scars that covered other parts of his body and all of his mind and thoughts, the scars that were part of the drinking.

The man in the mirror looked, stood, acted, smelled, and thought like a recruiting poster and was, above all things, a sergeant.

He turned away from the mirror and faced the room. He did not look at it or study it or glance at it—he faced it. Still straight and true, although beginning to weave slightly from left to right and front to back.

The room looked sterile.

The room looked like any of the hundred or so other barracks rooms he had lived in since he had left the small farm in Kansas eighteen years earlier. Everything in place, the bunk drum-tight, the shoes and boots beneath the bunk exactly in line and shined to flash the ceiling light. Locke was not one of those who bought patent leather shoes. He wore only issue clothing and spit-shined his shoes until they were black mirrors; just as he did not wear civilian clothes, only army issue uniforms, even when going off Fort Bliss for a night in Juárez, as he was now—because he was, above all things, a sergeant.

Against the wall by the right side of his bed stood a locker, closed but rigidly correct inside, with clothing hung in the prescribed manner, just as at the foot of his bunk in the foot locker were his underwear and shaving gear. At any given moment of any given day or night the room could be inspected and would pass with no gigs—demerits.

On the other side of the room from the locker stood a small gray table and a single chair. On the table, precisely in the center, stood a bottle of Cutty Sark Scotch whisky and a glass. It was the only thing—including Robert S. Locke—in the room that was not completely army issue.

He took two even strides forward, firmly grasped the bottle, and poured half a glass, which he swallowed, feeling the whiskey burn down his throat.

"Still not enough," he said aloud. "But coming, coming. . . ."

He put the bottle in the locker, wiped the glass with a bit of paper towel and set it next to the bottle, folded the paper scrap in a tiny rectangle and put it in his pocket to take with him and throw away later.

Once more he glanced around the room. It was ready—ready to be left.

He opened the door. As with all the other nights when he did not have night duty, this night Sergeant Robert S. Locke would go to Juárez, to the places where there would be noise and women and cheap whiskey that came from the bottle with a worm in it; and he would drink evenly and professionally until he was in a state that he called brain dead, which would last until he came back to the barracks and got ready for the next day.

He did this because if he did not do this, if he stayed in the room and waited for the next day, no matter how much he drank, they would come. His friends would come. All of his friends from all the battles would come in the moments when he least wanted them, come to visit him before he was properly brain dead and he could not stand that.

Above all he was a sergeant, but he could not stand that—could not stand his friends to come in the night.

So he closed the door firmly, the way the sergeant in the mirror would do it, with his back straight and his shoulders even, closed the door straight up and down. And the last thing he thought as he walked out of the barracks into the afternoon sun was the slogan from the recruiting ads on television:

"Be all you can be—join the army." Except he thought it the way they sang it. "Beeeee all that yooou can be, in the arrrmmmeeee."

3

*O*nce the Rio Grande had been a flowing river. It cut the desert sand between El Paso, Texas, and Juárez, Mexico, and defined the border. It was never mighty there, the way it is up north, near Taos, New Mexico, where it roars through canyons in white water—but once it had been a river.

Then they built dams on it up north, in New Mexico, and diverted the water for use in irrigation; now, when the water finally filters down to the space between El Paso and Juárez, it is nothing but a muddy trickle that makes filthy puddles in the litter and rocks of the border.

Still there is a large bridge; the Santa Fe Bridge covers the nearly dry riverbed arches up and over the rocks and mud and dirt, and all people entering Mexico in this area must walk or drive over the bridge.

Beneath it, between the two countries on any given day or night, there is a pack of ten to twenty children screaming at the tourists to throw money. At first, after the bridge was built some years ago but before the river was stolen by the northern farmers (as the Mexicans think of it), the boys would stand in waist-deep water and people would throw coins into the water to see them dive in the muck for pennies and nickels and sometimes a quarter. The water was fast then; and in the spring when the northern mountains fed it, there were eddies and currents that caught children, and some of them drowned.

As the river dried, it was thought the children would stop begging because there was no water to dive in, and tourists—it was believed—would only throw money to see them dive and swim and risk drowning. But then the tourists discovered that the children would fight over the money if enough was thrown. The amount varies, but gen-

erally if three or four quarters are thrown in a
scattered pattern it is enough to start things, and
the children will scrap in the mud and rocks and
litter, clawing each other and swearing to get the
small money. So now the same tourists who used
to watch the children risk drowning pay to see
them fight over change in the dry riverbed.

As an aid in catching the money many of the
children find sticks and poles and tie rough cardboard cones at the top, to try to snare the change
before it gets down into the rocks and mud and
broken glass; but the sticks also serve as weapons,
and the larger boys will use the money-catcher
sticks to whack the smaller boys out of the way
to get the falling money.

Manny hated the bridge, hated going to the
bridge, hated it because, as Maria had said, he
was smaller than many of the other boys and would
inevitably come away with some marks and lumps.
But early in the day it was the only way to get
money. Later, in the dark, he could make the
limp with his left leg and twist his right wrist to
make it look crippled. The soldiers would be getting drunk enough to feel sorry for him, and he
could perhaps get a little money begging. But this
night he would leave. He needed some money
now, and during the day the tourists were sober

and would not feel sorry for him—and so the bridge.

There were nearly half a dozen boys there when he arrived, even this early in the day, screaming at the few people crossing the bridge overhead.

"Come on—throw money! My mother is starving!"

"Throw money!"

"Throw money!"

Like Manny, many of the boys knew English well enough to hold a limited conversation with an American. They had learned it on the streets, had to learn it because it did no good to beg from other Mexicans—only Americans had money. Only Americans had enough extra money to throw it off a bridge. God, Manny thought—Dios, to have so much that you could just throw it off a bridge to see boys fight—to have that much money!

Two or three of the boys looked at Manny when he arrived, but they were all larger than he was so they didn't worry about him. He found a stick left by some other boy, and with a piece of cardboard he made his cone, wrapped it and tied and fastened it with a piece of scrap wire he had taken from an old banana box in back of the market.

He moved across the bridge, on the downriver side, opposite from where the other boys were begging. It was the bad side, the side where the tourists were going home and not coming over, but it was safer and he could work his way across when it looked good. He was small, he knew, but he was very fast, and that had saved him many times. He could run fast and dodge like an alley rat.

"Come on—throw money on this side! I am starving! See my ribs stick through my shirt!" Manny started his yell-chant, a rolling litany of sorrow that he would keep up for the entire time that he worked under the bridge. "Throw now— I will die if you do not throw money!"

Almost at once he saw a hand come over the side, and a coin fell. He caught it expertly in the cone and lowered it to find a quarter—a whole quarter!—and quickly glanced to see if the larger boys had seen it. He was lucky. One of them, an older boy he knew as Pacho but called many other things in his mind, who was as mean as snakes, had seen the coin fall; but there had been some coins at the same time on the other side of the bridge and he had gone for those. Manny turned away and expertly slid the coin into his mouth and under his tongue—it was not totally safe but the best place he had—and raised his cardboard catcher again.

"Throw money! Save me—save my mother and sister. Throw money!"

But none came for a time, although two soldiers leaned over to try and spit on him, laughing when he dodged, and he realized that he would have to move across the bridge.

He waited until the time was correct, when the other boys were busy yelling, then did it carefully. He moved to a position close to the Mexican side of the river—where the tourists rarely threw money—and then began sidling closer to the American side. He did not yell or appear to be pushy, but he knew that when they looked down the tourists liked his red hair and small appearance and would begin to throw money in his direction. It had worked many times and it worked now, but timing was critical. As soon as they saw he was getting money thrown to him, the other boys— especially Pacho—would swarm on him and take what he had gotten. If Manny did it correctly, he could get a couple of coins and run, skipping to dodge the aim of any rocks. If he waited a second too long, they would have him.

He waited too long.

Manny worked sideways to the other boys, ready always to fly. But a fat lady leaned over the side of the bridge and held out her hand, and there was a bill fluttering in it. Even far away it was possible to see that it was an American dollar, and all the boys' eyes were riveted on it. She let it go and the bill floated down, moving this way and that on small breezes, slipping one way and another to land as if drawn by a string to Manny's cone.

It was the best and worst possible thing that could happen. Manny pulled the cone down suddenly and the jerk caused the dollar to flop out. It was still within his reach and he grabbed for it, missed, grabbed again and caught it. But that half a second extra was too much and Pacho was on him like a street dog.

Two blows caught him, one in the stomach—which made him start to throw up the tortilla he'd gotten from Maria and also knocked the quarter out of his mouth—the second one to the side of his temple, which seemed to explode his whole brain in red flashes of color.

"Mestizo!" Pacho hissed at him. "Did you think I would let you keep the money?"

There was a flurry of blows now, expertly driven into his ribs to cause much pain and then, finally, as he lay on his face in the rocks and dirt, a final, viciously aimed kick to his groin.

Then there was nothing for a time, nothing but the pain below his stomach, and he heard the lady yelling that somebody should do something, somebody should help him, and he thought for a moment how silly the lady was to think anybody would come to help him. That was not the way of it under the bridge or anywhere else on the streets in Juárez. There was no help. Not for any was there help. They had a saying that even the priest would not help—he did not have time. Manny was lucky one of them had not used a knife on him, lucky he was alive after being stupid enough to get caught.

Then he stopped thinking of anything except that it was over: this was his last time because this night he was crossing. He could stand anything, take anything because this night he would cross to the north.

4

Sergeant Locke faced the door of the night-club the way he had faced his room in the barracks just before he left.

CLUB CONGO TIKI.

To enter the nightclub it was necessary to walk through the open mouth of the enormous head of a native with garishly painted palm trees on either side of the cheeks and lighted, giant teeth overhead.

It was, he decided the first time he came to the club, the ugliest place he had ever seen. So ugly, so incredibly ugly and in such poor taste that it was almost not real to him—almost a dream, the Congo Tiki—and that was why he came to it again and again. So much of what he was now, what he thought as he drank, was not real to him, that the club fit perfectly.

It was an insane place to go insane.

Just inside the door, to the left and right, there were large photo posters of two girls who were nearly nude. The one on the left had a sign across her middle that said simply GIRLS, hiding her body. The one on the right was covered with a carefully coiled and wrapped snake. It was a boa constrictor, or perhaps a pilated python—Robert could not be sure because he did not know for certain how to tell the difference—but it was a real snake. He knew that because every night he watched the two ladies dance to the brassy music, the loud, grinding clanky music; they would dance and almost but not quite reveal parts of their bodies, and every night the snake hung there, its tongue flicking in and out while the lady on the right danced.

One night a soldier had been loud in the second performance and had said something insulting about the snake and the lady. She had jumped off the runway in the center of the club and put the snake on his table with a thump and the snake had crawled hastily into the soldier's lap. The soldier was young and from somewhere like Iowa where they didn't have large snakes. His tongue had stuck to the roof of his mouth with fear and his eyes had grown large and white and he had passed out and made a mess. Robert had smiled for days, remembering the way the soldier had gurgled trying to form words with his tongue stuck to the roof of his mouth.

So he knew it was a real snake, and in a way that fit with the rest of the club because it was insane for a woman to dance wearing nothing but a boa constrictor or a pilated python for clothing, insane to dance that way in a club named the Congo Tiki where you walked through the mouth of a giant native with lighted teeth. And it all helped him to leave the real world and disappear into the dream world he thought he needed—the dream world where he didn't have to worry about his old friends coming to call.

It was, finally, perfect, because he did not really come to see the ladies dance without their clothes but came just to get drunk. He was probably the only person who came just for that, just to drink. He would take a table back in the corner each night, not down near the runway where most of the soldiers sat, and he would tell the waiter not to bring him the watered whiskey they usually served but the stronger pure Scotch, and he would work professionally—a sergeant all the way—at obliterating his normal thought processes. He worked to get drunk the same way he would work at taking an objective.

Start here and go to there—nothing in the way could stop him.

During the first week that he came to the Congo Tiki, when he was first assigned to Fort Bliss, Texas, from Fort Sill, Oklahoma, they had pushed all the other things at him. The girls would come to sit with him and touch him to make him buy drinks for them, buy the tea water that looked like drinks so they could get the money from him and perhaps get more than that later. But when he made it obvious that he didn't want more than to drink alone, and when he paid them to leave and not drink, they felt a kind of pity for him and left him.

It had been months now—how many? Seven, eight months, and they left him alone. Sometimes a new girl would try him, a new young girl in from the barrios on the outskirts of Juárez where it was said that anything you did, anywhere you could go in the world would be better than there—sometimes one of them would sit at his table and touch him in the way that meant so little but seemed to mean so much and try to get him to buy her a drink; but he would simply look at her the way the person in the mirror would look at her, with the look of a line sergeant, and she would move away.

That was not part of his life now. Nothing was part of his life now but the drinking, the making of the fog to blind all other things.

He moved out of the afternoon light in the doorway into the darkness of the interior and went to his usual table back in the corner. There would be nothing for two or three hours—no dancing, no music, no other soldiers—and that would give him time to get a proper start.

The waiter brought him a drink without his ordering it and he sat quietly in the dark, sipping it, waiting. Once he had known a lieutenant in an infantry unit who actually liked it, liked what the infantry meant—the smell of it, the rattle of it, the fire and manuever, the cover and assault. He thought of himself as all man, that lieutenant, and would spit and swear with the men and smoke in the John Wayne way (before John Wayne died of cancer), smoking the cigarette in the two-fisted macho way so it hung in the side of his mouth.

In fact he had been smoking a cigarette that way the day he died when he got caught by an AK-47 burst at the edge of a small hamlet in Vietnam. The burst had carried him back and down into the side of a hooch, and he was instantly dead and so did not become part of the friends who came to call on Robert, but the cigarette stayed in the corner of his mouth even in death until one of the men reached over and pulled it out and stepped on it. For all of that the lieutenant was a phony and the men knew it. They knew he was a phony because when he drank he sipped his whiskey in tiny little sips and did not use it hard and fast to wipe his mind as the men, the real men, did.

Robert could not sip a drink now without at least once thinking of the lieutenant who was not a man. He thought perhaps that he was also not a man, not a man in the way the lieutenant had wanted to be a man—a man who could spit and swear with the men and knock a drink back. Robert could spit and swear well enough, but he didn't smoke—hated the smell of it—and had always sipped his drinks, even after it had become necessary to drink to brain death.

He sipped because he had to wait, and if you knocked it back you could not wait. He had to wait for the fog that came because if he didn't wait, if he drank too fast and was a man like the lieutenant wanted to be, the fog would not come. And instead of becoming brain dead he would awaken the ghosts of his friends and they would come. Oh, they would come, and he could not stand that, could not live with that.

It was a very complicated process, Robert's use and abuse of alcohol, very devious and complicated, and he suspected strongly that it meant he was not a true macho man, and that made him a little sad but not too much. Most of the true macho men he knew or had known were dead. Just as all the heroes, the true heroes, were dead.

And he was not—except for his brain.

All a very complicated way to stay alive, if not macho, and so he sat at the corner table and sipped his drink and thought briefly of the lieutenant, and that made him think of the heat of Vietnam— the incredible heat that was not believable and the smell of the heat in Vietnam, the smell that had a copper taste and the copper taste that became fear all from the heat.

He sat at the corner table and sipped and waited to go insane for this night.

Later the club would fill with young soldiers and some older sergeants, although no officers would come. They had their own clubs. The young soldiers would sit at the tables close to the runway and they would drink the watered tequila and whiskey and make rude noises and gestures, louder and louder as they began to think they were drunk, feeling all the strength of what they were. Later that would happen and two or three or four of them would snort and fight and scream as young animals might, and they would yell at the dancers until finally somebody—one of the new ones—would climb up on the runway and reach for a dancer. Then the bouncer, a gentle giant of a man who was named Martinez and spoke no English and could hold a soldier absolutely still, like a kitten, without hurting him, would stop them and things would settle for the night.

From then on there would be the brassy music from the four-horn-and-one-guitar band and the smell of sweat from the girls dancing and the indescribable odor from the toilet—just a trench in concrete in a back room—and the night would pass until Robert was brain dead and insane and would go into the alley in back of the club to throw up because he could not stand the toilet.

Then he would head back to Fort Bliss on the city bus from the bridge, dozing in his seat, and get cleaned up for another day of work as a man who was, above all things, a sergeant.

He sipped his drink and waited.

5

Manny sat in the dark and waited.

He was near the river in a broken corner of an old building that was not used, tucked into a crumbled piece of cement culvert tubing, hiding with his mouth closed so his teeth would not show and his eyes squinted to cover the whites. A creature of the night, safe—he thought of himself as a Night Animal. It was hard to be safe on the river at night.

It was hard to be safe anywhere in Juárez at night, but on the river in the darkness it was doubly difficult. At first hard dark, the people who would cross in the night started to gather. Hundreds of them would congregate in groups and singles with small bags of clothing and food and wait in the rocks of the Mexican side for when it seemed right. On the other side of the river there was a fence, but it was down and broken in many places; and the American border patrol had lights as well, large floodlights, but people who would cross threw rocks until these were broken and the border was in tight darkness except for the faint glow from the club lights on the strip in Juárez. But it was not these people who made it unsafe. Nor was it the American border patrol, although they were large and could be mean if they wanted to be mean. It was the others.

It was sometimes the coyotes—the people who took others across for money and promised them safety and lied. Not all of them, but some of them lied and would steal from the people they said they were going to help. Enough of them did that—stole from them and took money and more from the women and sometimes even killed them—so that it was not safe to be near a group. There was not a way to know if the coyote for that group would be evil.

But still worse than the coyotes were the street

men, the vultures who worked the streets after dark came, with knives and with cords and with the pointed boots that kicked—the evil ones who would cut and kill for nothing. For the smell of it. Those were the worst. More than once they had nearly taken Manny to be sold only to have him slip away, pull and run and use his speed to hide in the night.

After it was truly dark they came down into the river and struck like wild dogs against the groups of people waiting for it to be safe to cross to the north. Always in silence they struck, sometimes with small hot laughs if they found women or found somebody with even a small amount of money or good boots to steal. So vicious were they that it was almost unnecessary for them to do evil—just the threat of what they would do usually got them what they wanted.

They were the true danger.

They were the reason it was not safe in the river and there was nobody to help the people. What police there were in Juárez were too busy taking care of themselves to worry about illegal crossers in the dark, and the American police or border patrol did not care if they were hurt or used or killed. It just meant fewer who crossed for them to try to catch, fewer to capture and handcuff and take to the holding pens to wait for the buses that would take them back to Mexico. . . .

So Manny waited in the night, the Night Animal waited and listened to the sounds: hurried whispers, people giving each other courage for the run. Nobody knew for sure when to start crossing, but sometime after midnight some people closer to the bridge started across; and that triggered a wave, a whole wave of them, and they began running.

Manny held back. Before coming he had gone by the Two-by-Four, and Maria had given him a chicken and five tortillas in a paper sack. He thought of them now, held against his stomach in two fists, and he decided to wait.

Nobody knew for sure how the border patrol worked the American side of the border, because they changed their tactics often. One night they would wait in one place, all together, the next time they would be in another or spread out, and they never did the same thing twice. But Manny had a plan. He reasoned that when the main groups started across, the border patrol would be waiting and would capture many of them, but Manny thought they would have to leave with the ones they captured, to take them to the holding areas.

There might be a chance then, when they were gone, for Manny to slip across alone. In the meantime he was hungry, and if he waited to eat the chicken and got caught he might not get to eat it. It would be better to eat a little now, just in case. . . .

He opened the sack and let the smell of the garlic from the chicken take him. He reached in and pulled a leg and thigh off the chicken—cooked so that it nearly fell off the bird—then took a tortilla and stripped meat from the bones and wrapped the meat in the tortilla and ate it in three bites.

He could not believe how good it was—better by far than that time when he was small and had the five American dollars. Oh now, he thought, now this is too good to leave; all his resolve left him, and he ate and ate until the chicken was gone—the bones cleaned and sucked dry, his fingers licked until the taste was gone, all the flour-dusty corn tortillas gone, sitting there in the darkness while the others crossed, and he was just finishing when the lights came on.

The border patrol had set up enormous spotlights on the other side, hidden between buildings and garbage dumpsters, and four or five of them—it was impossible to tell exactly how many in the sudden explosion of light—came on at the same time, aimed down into the river. For a full three seconds the river was a frozen sea of people. Hundreds, perhaps a thousand of them were caught in the glaring blue-white, and they stopped for that time, hesitated in silence, huddled in the slashing light like mice. Then the border patrol triggered loudspeakers and an announcement blared out in Spanish that all of them were caught and they should either move back across the river or lie face down with their hands in back of their heads.

Of course no people did as they were asked. Everybody started running and screaming at once, some back but the vast majority of them running for the United States side of the river, defying the border patrol, ignoring the commands, pouring up the banks of the river like a living flood of people.

The announcement repeated itself—it seemed to be a recording fed into an amplifier system— and on the other side of the lights Manny could see the dim figures of runners being captured by teams of border patrol. Some of them were captured. But most of them ran through the border patrol, screaming and pulling until they were gone in the night—just too many for the small team of officers to capture.

There was much noise and swearing, and for a time it seemed that Manny's plan might work. The lights remained on, filling the river with day, but the border patrol had to leave with the crowds of people they had arrested. Manny crouched in the culvert and thought if he waited just a bit more he could slide sideways down the river to the end of the lighted area and get across.

He started to move, easing backward out of his cubbyhole, when a hand grabbed him by the hair.

"Ahh, what is this?" a sharp voice said. "What kind of rabbit hides here?"

Manny swiveled his head around, pulling against the hair, and felt the fear rise in him. There was always some fear—but it came now almost as a sickness, to make his legs weak and his heart skip a beat.

There were four of them, four of the street wolves who wore leather jackets in the night even though it was hot, their shirts open to their waists and the sharp pointed black boots and long hair. Manny knew them, not by name, but he had seen them in the streets hunting, looking for small ones, weak ones.

Looking for Manny. Boys like Manny.

"Did you think you could cross?" The one holding him pulled Manny to his feet with his hair, twisting and jerking at the same time until it seemed Manny's hair would pull his scalp off. "Was it that way with you? Did you think you could leave Mexico and go live with the gringos?"

One of the others reached over and slapped him. "Don't you like us? Don't you like living with us in Mexico?"

Manny said nothing. Fear had been replaced by thought, by all the cunning that had kept him moving and safe on the streets. Talk was for nothing. Now he must think and be ready to act. Twice today he had been stupid. Once at the bridge, when he waited for the paper money, and now, caught in the lights like a fool. He thought hotly, fiercely, that if he got out of this he would never be caught again, never be foolish or stupid again.

If he got away.

"I have seen him on the streets before, near the back of the Two-by-Four, begging. He is the little red-haired one."

"Raoul would like him," the one in the back said, stepping forward. "Raoul has said that he would pay for a small boy such as this—and one with red hair. That will bring more. Do not rip his hair out—Raoul will pay more for the hair."

His chance came then. Just as the one holding him eased off a tiny fraction the searchlights went out. It was so sudden—the jump from the white-hot light to the deep blackness of the riverbed—that nothing could be seen. In that second, in the momentary blindness, Manny kicked as hard as he could up between the legs of the man holding him and was rewarded with a guttural scream and the hand releasing his hair.

He ran down the river at first without thinking. He could see nothing and tripped and fell, scrambled to his feet, tripped and fell again, and once more came up running, now clawing up the bank, knowing only that if they caught him—the screaming, swearing ones who chased him in the wild night—if they caught him now, nothing, not even the money from Raoul, would save him. And it was in this way that he first met the sergeant.

6

Alleys in Juárez are not made with sense. Sometimes there will be an alley in back of a shop or bar, and again there might be just a narrow, winding pathway littered with drunks and garbage. Often an alley will seem to start and then just end with a wall, where somebody has decided to build another building without any special care given to planning.

To escape into the alleys, as Manny now started to do, was at best a dangerous thing to try. The four men were fast, and anger drove them still

faster, and they knew the alleys as well as Manny.
But Manny was driven by something deeper than
anger—all that he was wanted to survive.

Up from the river he ran, between two buildings where there was a slot just wide enough for
his shoulders. He careened through, bouncing from
one side to the other, and found himself on a
lighted street. People were everywhere, but it was
not good to be in the light. They would see him.

He pushed through a couple of tourists—a man
and a woman who were wearing large hats and
serapes and swore at him—and tore off down the
sidewalk. He heard the tourists swear again as the
first of his pursuers hit them. Close, too close. He
did not turn to look but they were nearly on him.

Traffic in the street was heavy, with cars bumper
to bumper and nearly stopped. He cut left and
went over the hood of an old Chevrolet turned
into a taxi—catching another curse from the driver
that would have embarrassed his mother had he
known her—then across the sidewalk and between two more buildings.

He could hear their boots slapping the ground
now, but he was gaining slightly. Manny knew
this area. There was a dark alley in back of this
row, with a dead end on the left, but a stack of
crates lay against the low wall. If he went to the

right he would come out on the street again, but if he moved left he could scrabble over the boxes and perhaps get away.

He grabbed the corner of the building to pull himself around and into the alley. The boxes were as he thought, and he hardly slowed as he pulled himself over them and to the top of the alley wall. As an afterthought he kicked the boxes back down into a heap and slipped over the wall to drop in the space next to another building. They would not get him now.

He kept up the pace and ran once more out into a lighted street full of people. It was getting late now, two or three in the morning, and even Juárez began to slow in the tired hours. He ran down two more blocks, slipped sideways another block, and slowed to a walk, watching the streets in back, weaving through people slowly.

It was not a good night. He was away from them, but all of the rest of this night was not good. He had not crossed and could not do so now—it was too close to light. He had made all his fine words and brave songs about leaving, crowing like a stupid young rooster, had told Maria and had gotten the chicken and her sad eyes, and now he was still here, still in Juárez. He hurt from the roots of his hair where the pig had held him—

he had also lost his cap with Ford on it—to his ribs and lower areas from the battle under the bridge.

It had not been a good day and now he was tired. No, more than tired, he was weak with it, ready to collapse with the need for sleep and rest, and it was two more blocks over to his cardboard lean-to near the church. He decided not to go all the way but to find a doorway to doze in. He crossed the street and went into an alley that ran in back of the Club Congo Tiki.

It was not as dark in this alley, and there were door openings for sleeping. But before he had taken ten steps he saw a figure leaning against the wall in back of the club.

It was an American soldier. Tall, filled out but tall, he was leaning with both hands against the wall throwing up all the liquor he had spent good money on. Manny shook his head. It was like the ones who tossed the money off the bridge. To have that kind of money, to have enough to throw off a bridge or to drink just to vomit it up in an alley!

Manny stopped, waited. He was going to wait until the soldier was done, then move farther down the alley. But the thought came then—a small thought. Here was a man who was so drunk he did not know where he was, so drunk he could only lean against the wall and vomit. In a dark alley the man was doing this, right there, right in front of Manny.

And so the thought.

It might be that I can slip up in back of him, Manny thought. It might be that I can move on him like a Night Animal and reach into his pocket and get his wallet.

Even in the dark he could see the bulge of a wallet in the soldier's back pocket.

There would be money there. Money that would be only for throwing off a bridge or vomiting up in an alley. Money for Manny to eat. Money to make up for this day, perhaps money to make up for many horrible days. American soldiers always had money; money to help Manny cross to the north, to buy more food; money to perhaps buy even a belt with a large buckle or a hat.

All of it right there, in the back pocket of the man leaning against the wall losing all of the expensive tequila. It might be so that I can just slip there and put my hand in the pocket and get the wallet and he will not know.

It is not stealing, Manny thought—he will only spend it on something to throw up anyway. I can just move in the darkness this way on the side of the building and reach out from the side this way and carefully, oh so carefully put my hand in his pocket this way . . . ahh, see the bulging wallet so full of money. So full. . . .

Manny's hand hovered over the pocket while Robert Locke hunched and made sick sounds. Manny waited until the time was right, perfectly right, and let two fingers slide gently down, into the opening of the pocket.

"Damn." It was not loud or even surprised-sounding. Just the simple word and Robert's hand shot back off the wall and wrapped Manny's wrist in an iron hard hold. "What's this?"

Manny could not believe the strength in the grip. He had seen many soldiers drunk, had begged money from them, but this one was different. To come off the wall in that manner—the hand so fast even with him so drunk he could hardly stand—to come that fast and hold him now like some trap, to hold him this way—was not possible. Here was more power than all four of the men who had chased him. Here was more power to hold him than he could have imagined, all the power in the world in the one strong hand that held him, dangling by one arm as he fought and twisted, while Robert finished vomiting, backed away from the wall, cleaned himself.

The hand held while all of that happened, held while Manny cursed and fought silently, held with all of the stinking, fat, bridge-throwing-money-owning-puking power that the Americans could have. The hand clamped and held.

Then Robert, without speaking further, started walking down the alley to the street, the hand still locked on Manny as if belonging to some other person, some other sergeant. The sergeant in the mirror.

"What is this?" Manny hissed. "What are you doing to me?"

Robert said nothing, kept walking, stumbling slightly with the drink still but not too drunkenly. He had thrown off much of it, had made another night, and now needed only the bus and the doze and the barracks and another day running his squad of good men. He tried to remember their names as he walked down the alley but could not. They were good men, he thought, but he could never remember their names. Which was just as well. It was best to not remember their names. . . .

"Are you mad?" Manny held back, jerking, but could do nothing to slow the sergeant. "No, wait— are you one of those?" He made his voice take the insult sound he knew from the streets of Juárez.

"Are you one who takes boys? A soldier who takes boys?"

Still Robert said nothing. He reached the street and turned to walk to the bridge, the small figure kicking and fighting at his side. There was the thought that as long as he held them—that's how Robert thought of Manny—as long as he held them and didn't let them go, they could never steal from him or take him or hurt him.

Robert walked down the street, moving through the people. There were fewer now in the morning than before, mostly drunk men moving toward the bridge to get back to their units, and the ladies who had spent another night earning a living were coming into the streets to go back to the barrios and huts and boxes on the outside of Juárez— where they could not live but had families waiting for them—and the people who cleaned the bars and clubs and pits were getting ready for the next night of tourists and soldiers. Robert moved through all of this with Manny in his hand, and nobody stopped him. Inside it was Robert moving through the people, but outside it was the sergeant in the mirror dragging a Mexican boy, a straight up and down sergeant who had seen and been and done, and there were not many who would want to stop him just to ask about the boy he was dragging.

It was two blocks to the bridge, and by the end of the first block Manny stopped struggling and followed. There was not a way for him to break the grip. The marching man owned him, was taking him wherever he wished, and it could be, he thought smiling as they neared the bridge, it could be that he would drag Manny across and just keep going, heading north. It could be that Manny would cross this night still. . . .

As they neared the Mexican side of the bridge, where the sidewalk narrows into a walkway, a Mexican policeman stepped out. He looked as all Juárez policemen look—khaki uniform only slightly wrinkled, leather gunbelt with a silver-plated, pearl-handled .45 automatic pistol in a holster, hat back on his head, slight paunch, legs a bit apart; and as with police in all places not any show of softness or weakness, all hard and power to control the situation. Manny had not seen him, but he suddenly appeared at the point where the sidewalk narrows. He smiled at the sergeant.

"Are you taking a little too much home, sergeant?"

Robert stopped, only slightly confused. Then he looked down at Manny as if seeing him for the first time. Still he did not let go but held Manny in a locked grip. "Who are you?"

Maybe he would tell about the wallet. . . . Manny turned to the policeman. "He is of those who like boys. He is kidnapping me. Make him release me."

The policeman had been in Juárez, working the streets starting at midnight, for nearly twelve years. Nothing surprised him. Nothing. He had heard all possible lies from all possible sources about all possible things. Sometimes, when there was time and he was bored, he would mix them up, take lies from one source and mix them with subjects from another, about situations from yet another. He looked at the large sergeant and stepped back a pace to give himself room and time if he needed to react suddenly. His hand automatically went nearer the holster. "Is this true? Are you taking the boy against his will?"

Where was it, Robert thought, where was it that this happened before? The alcohol made his lips numb. The alcohol made his head numb. The alcohol made the whole world numb.

"Let go of the boy, señor."

Where was it? Was it in Saigon? No, somewhere else. It was somewhere else. He was standing, holding somebody by the wrist for something, and somebody ordered him to release the person—oh, yes. That had been in El Salvador. No, Honduras. Wait—where was it? Somewhere . . .

"Release the boy and step back, senor." The smile was gone, had been replaced by an even look that could go either way, to courtesy or death. The policeman unhooked the safety strap on the holster, and his hand rested openly on the butt of the gun. "Release the boy and put your hands on your head. Now!"

Hell, Robert thought. It had been Kansas City when he was there on detachment. A kid had started to run in front of a car and he had caught him by the wrist. A Kansas City policeman had told him to let the kid go and he had done it. He looked at Manny and released him.

Manny started to run off, but the policeman stopped him with a palm up. In Juárez the police have ultimate, complete power. A mere wave can condemn or save you. "I wish to learn the truth of all this."

"It is as I said," Manny rushed. "He was taking me back against my will. . . ." Another gesture and he was silent.

"What do you say?" The policeman looked at

Robert Locke. "What is your story of this? Why were you dragging the boy?"

The fog cleared and Robert remembered Manny trying to get his wallet. He started to say something about it, then realized if he did the police would come down on Manny. Skinny kid, he thought—arm felt like it was going to break. Like leathery, brittle wood. "He was guiding me to the bridge. I forgot where it was, and when I saw it I just started to drag him with me. I've had some to drink. . . ."

The policeman sighed. All lies. It was the only absolute that he knew. All people lied about all things all the time. After a time you did not look for the truth any longer but simply tried to manage the lies and keep things moving correctly. In this case the lie would work. The boy was not hurt and was probably lying, had probably tried to steal from the sergeant; the sergeant was drunk but did not want trouble and could make bad trouble, judging by the size of his shoulders and the set of his eyes and neck, if he was pushed too far (the policeman was an expert on trouble with soldiers). This particular lie would manage nicely, the policeman thought. He waved Manny away, and he was gone before

Robert was aware of it. Then the policeman pointed with his chin to the bridge, the border, and smiled Robert on his way and that was the first meeting between Manny and the sergeant.

THE
SECOND
MEETING

7

In the usual flow of his life things had to work very fast for Manny or not at all. If he begged and got money from a tourist or soldier, it had to happen fast because if larger boys saw him get the money they would move in and either take his money or muscle him out of the way and ruin any chance he had of getting further money from the turista.

So fast. In order to live he could not have leisure time, time to study a thing slowly or do it at his own pace. He would be working down the side of the street limping, one hand clawed to perfection in the attitude of the begging cripple, and he would see a turista—the best kind were the men who came to drink and see women take their clothes off because they did not care for their money so much—and he had only moments to impress on the turista that he would die without the money, would die without the rich American money and help.

So fast. And because he had to live so fast, he could not take time to learn a thing the way it should be learned. If somebody told him a thing, he had to take that thing at face value, had to live with that thing as he was told it was, because if he took the time to study it and see if it was true he would starve. Of course he starved anyway or was always on the edge of starving; but if he did not beg for a day or work the edges of the market the way a dog works at a butcher shop, he would truly starve and become weak and perhaps sick, and there was nothing for him then if that happened. There was not a person who would take care of him and he would then die—which had happened to some boys that he knew; they had gotten thinner and thinner and then died in sickness or hunger in the alleys and had been found by the police.

So fast he had to be that he could not learn, but he had one thing, one thing that he knew to be a fact because there was proof of it. Three blocks off to the side of the street from the bridge was the market, and one block over from the market were the railroad tracks coming into Juárez from southern Mexico. Near the tracks was the bullring and next to the bullring was the Rio Brava Hotel, and it was there that Pancho Villa came when he took the city, came on horses up the tracks to take the city. Manny knew it was true because the places where his bullets struck were still there in the brick walls of the hotel.

In the mornings, in the early mornings when he awakened under the cardboard and the light was just coming to bring the stink-heat of the day, he would sometimes go to work the market. Set in a whole block, closed in over the top, the market was dozens of stalls and cubicles crammed in with curtains over them, all selling all the things there were to sell in Juárez. Food—goat cheeses that were soft and rubbery and smelled still of the goats, the thick smell of them, and tortillas cooked on iron burners much like Maria's in the Two-by-Four, and burritos with meat said to come from the bullring but covered with chopped red peppers so hot it didn't matter about the meat, thick cones of sugar candy, the iced drinks with the dirty ice that smelled of the streets but was not bad for all that, and vegetables laid in open crates with the owner waving a feathered whisk over them to keep the clouds of flies from landing. And shops full of metal-enamel dishes and spoons, pots to cook food in if one had food, racks full of clothing and other racks with leather boots and belts covered with flowers and a blank place for the name. The market.

Just at dawn he would come to the market, and before they opened sometimes he would go onto the railroad tracks near the bullring and Rio Brava Hotel to stand and look down the tracks and think what it must have been like. They would have come here, he would think—just in this way they would have ridden into town and up the tracks, the horses all across and thundering, the men in their sombreros with the chin straps and the leather pants, carrying their silver pistols in their hands, shooting this way and that—to own and be, to have the power of the silver pistols just as the police now had the power of the silver pistols and they would shoot in this manner—he would hold his hand up, the finger extended—and the bullets would come to the wall of the Rio Brava Hotel and take the brick, *shuueee*, in this manner.

What a thing it was then, he thought. What a thing to see it must have been. All the horses coming in abreast and the men firing and Pancho in front with his large sombrero and the silver pistol, and it was said he also had a silver saddle and a large mustache and the strength of five men. To have seen him then, coming up the tracks at the head of his men, taking Juárez—ahh, to have seen that would have been something. Twice now he had thought of changing his name to Pancho— of taking the new name to honor the man with the silver pistols, just as he had taken the name Manny to honor a Mañuel who had been a prizefighter when he was very small and living in back of the church. Mañuel the fighter, Mañuel Bustos, had been strong in this manner, strong like Pancho Villa had been, must have been. . . .

Just at dawn he must have come, as Manny came to see it at dawn, and he wished that he could know more of this thing with Pancho Villa and how he took the city, just as he wished he could know more of southern Mexico. Every day the train left Juárez and headed south, the beautiful silver train with the bubbles on top where the people could sit and ride and see the country in such a manner, such a manner as to be rich, and Manny watched them leave. They went the same way as Pancho Villa had come to leave his bullet marks in the hotel; the trains went south, and Manny knew nothing of them after they were out of sight as he knew nothing of Pancho except the bullet marks, but there was not time to learn.

There was only time to see the bullet marks and think of Pancho Villa and see the trains leave and wonder—only time to wonder. Then he would go to the market, when the stalls started to open, and work them as a dog works the butcher shops, working around the edges. It was not good to beg at the market because those who worked in the stalls did not want beggars because of what they did to business. People did not want to buy as much when small boys were begging, and at first, when he discovered working the market, Manny used this knowledge. He would beg, knowing the stall people did not like it, and sometimes they would pay him with a dark banana or a broken piece of candy to leave and not hurt their business. But after a time they knew that he knew what he was doing, and they started to convince him not with bananas or candy but thumping blows across his back; and Manny had to find another way to use the market.

That was when he discovered the butcher shop

dogs. At the back of the market was the shop for meat, which Manny did not usually try because it was not good to get things he had to cook. All the meat in the shop was raw, and he could not cook anything. Once he had tried eating meat raw but became ill and so did not do it any longer. But the meat smell brought the street dogs of Juárez. It brought flies as well, clouds of them all around the shop, but always there were two or three dogs. And Manny wondered about them as much as he wondered about Pancho Villa and the silver trains.

The dogs could not live. Manny lived only barely on what he could find, and there wasn't anything else for the dogs, nothing, and yet they lived. So he watched them, watched one black-and-white dog in particular. This dog did not fight or snap like the others when the butcher threw a piece of meat into the alley because it had been blown with fly eggs and they had hatched into the small white worms, or the fat had gone too green. The other dogs tore at it and would start fighting, but this one, the black-and-white one, hung back and watched from the edges; and when the time was right he moved in and got the meat or fat.

Always.

It was a way to be, Manny thought, a way to

get something from the stalls, and the next morning he came to the market when they opened and hung back and watched the stall keepers begin cleaning the stalls; and when the time was right he would step forward and help. Not really to help, but to be seen, to be seen correctly. He would pick up a piece of trash and put it in the trash container or help to fold the curtain that had covered the produce for the night to keep the flies out, and they would often give him something. A dark banana or broken piece of sugared candy or a soft peach—the same things he used to get by begging when they wanted him to leave, except that now he could stay and work all the stalls this way and get enough food sometimes to hold him for the whole day. . . .

Not often that much, but sometimes enough for a day. And it was on a Saturday morning when he came to work the market edges that the second meeting occurred.

It seemed like nothing when it started. Saturdays were the best day to come to the market because it was then that the new produce came in for the week, as well as the new cheeses, and those in the stalls would select the worst that had not sold during the week to take home for themselves. And there was a generosity in them, especially if the week had not gone too badly, and Manny could get extra bananas or vegetables.

He had done this and had been lucky. He had gotten a full tomato still almost all red, full and rich and wet, and celery and some carrots and a piece of goat cheese as big as his fist with only a thin film of mold. There were other boys in the market on Saturday, so he went outside in the rear, walking the block over to the tracks to eat his breakfast in peace, when he looked up and saw the tall American sergeant walking across the tracks and heading for the Rio Brava Hotel.

Manny recognized him instantly, though it had been night when he last saw the tall sergeant. He stepped back in a doorway, but the sergeant did not look at him. It was still very early, with few people moving, and the sergeant—Manny could see that he was drunk but in control—stepped briskly up to the hotel steps and disappeared inside.

And now a strange thing happened.

Always before Manny worked on the side of speed and caution. If he took risks it was because that was the only way to live, but always there was caution; now caution left him and the thought came that he should go to the hotel and see what the sergeant was doing.

8

The Rio Brava Hotel was set so that when you came in the manager's desk was to the right, the stairs up to the rooms were to the left, and straight ahead was the hotel café—an open, sunny room always dirty and full of noise and people and the smells of Mexican cooking. It was not a hotel the turistas came to but one used by people coming from the south to Juárez on business, to sell in the market or go to one of the many dentists or opticians or divorce parlors. A no-nonsense hotel, old and full of dust and people.

Manny walked in the front door slowly. He had only been inside the hotel twice. Once to see if he could beg—before he knew there were no turistas—and the second time to try for food at the café. Both times the man at the desk had thrown him out and he did not really expect to get away with it this time, but the desk manager was not there.

He saw the sergeant sitting at a table in the rear of the café, alone; and, thinking that he should not be doing this, that he should turn and leave, Manny walked into the café. The waiter, a man in jeans and a dirty white shirt, saw him come in and would have thrown him out, but he had a plate of eggs for a side table and only hissed a warning to Manny, which the boy ignored. There was this, he thought—the sergeant had covered for him with the police, had not told the police of his attempt to steal the wallet, and that might mean the sergeant was generous. If he was generous there might be a further chance to beg. All of this was in Manny's thinking, but it was not what brought him into the hotel and into the café. He was drawn to the sergeant by something else, something that made him want to know more of the sergeant, and he walked to the sergeant's table and stood, silent, watching him.

Robert did not at first see the boy. He had taken

the table in the corner with his back to the wall just as he always tried to find tables in corners against walls. The waiter had not come yet, and he was looking at the menu. He could not read Spanish but understood simple things—eggs were *huevos*, coffee was *café*, milk was *leche*, and it did not matter anyway. He was here to eat because he must eat, not because he liked food, and he would do as he usually did—order the first thing at the top of the menu and hope that it did not have *menudo* in it because that was tripe, and he did not eat tripe because it was guts; and although it was eaten to cure hangovers, he did not have a hangover because he was still drunk—and he looked up from the menu to see a boy standing there.

Red hair, skinny-brittle arms, dressed in dirty clothes so large on him the shirt seemed to wrap around the front. No cap. No, he thought, correct that—in the service it was said that a man without a cap did not have cover. The boy had no cover. Strange way to put it, he thought, and wondered why so many things in the army were strange and seemed to be without meaning. A cap was a cover. Shoes were not shoes but low-quarters. Call everything what it wasn't and change what it was. . . .

To kill was to interdict. Eliminate positions. Neutralize.

Bright red hair. Some red-haired soldier for a father perhaps. Standing that way, with that upside-down look on his face—the look that could be either a smile or a frown depending on which way Robert looked at it—he knew he had seen the boy before, oh yes. Where was that now? Was it him, was it Robert who had seen the red-haired boy or was it the man in the mirror, who did not always tell him what he had seen, could not always tell him?

Was it Fort Ord? No, that wasn't a boy; it was a woman with red hair. Long hair that had been, long hair that fell and fell like soft, wounded rain, in whorls that went around her shoulders, white shoulders, and she had cried, the woman, cried and cried when Robert had to leave . . . no. Not Fort Ord but somewhere like that or maybe not, too, but somewhere with red hair, and then it came into his mind without his meaning it to and he saw the bridge and the Mexican policeman and remembered holding the skinny arm and that the boy had tried to steal his wallet in the alley, and he smiled. Robert smiled and said, "Hello."

Manny nodded but said nothing. He was chewing on a piece of celery, having put the moldy goat cheese in his pocket for later, and wondering why the sergeant took so long to speak to him or tell him to leave. The waiter came up in back of Manny and took hold of his shirt and started to drag him away, saying in Spanish that he wasn't allowed, and the sergeant looked at the waiter and said:

"No."

The waiter stopped because it was not Robert who said it but the man in the mirror and it was not a statement but a proclamation—this thing that was happening would not happen any longer, just as quiet thunder proclaimed rain. It was done. Just *No* and it was done. The waiter released Manny and stood at his side, looked at the sergeant and smiled and apologized and asked if the sergeant was ready to order.

Robert said nothing to the waiter but looked at Manny. "I was about to have breakfast. Would you like to join me?"

Manny did not know all English words, or even many of them, but the ones he understood, the useful ones, were enough for him to understand what Robert was saying and more; and he also knew the opportunity to eat was here, to eat real food. He slid forward into the chair and nodded.

Robert handed him the menu, and there was a

problem now because Manny had never learned to make sense of words on paper. He stared at the menu for a moment as if considering it, then looked up at the waiter and said that he wanted some eggs and some meat, perhaps a steak, with a large bowl of frijoles and a plate of tortillas on the side and a large glass of orange juice without ice and a bowl of those small biscuits covered with the white sugar like flour and a pitcher of cold water and some of those boiled potatoes and a plate of chopped sausage—and he stopped to take a breath.

The waiter looked at the sergeant with a question in his eyes. Robert nodded and Manny continued.

He also wanted two burritos (he thought he could carry them for later) and a rolled-up tube of sweetmeats and a shaker of ground chili powder for the eggs. Finally he was done simply because he could not think of anything more without going to look at the back of the counter, and he was worried that if he got up to look, the sergeant would change his mind.

Robert ordered two eggs and a glass of tomato juice and nothing more. Edges were there, sharp edges were starting to show in his thinking; and he had the whole weekend, until Monday morning, before he had to be back at Fort Bliss, and he did not want edges. Food would make the edges sharper, and he would not have anything to drink until he went to the liquor store near the bridge, so he had to eat light.

The boy sat and watched him as if expecting something—something other than the food. Talk? Did he expect Robert to talk to him? How very strange that would be. He did not talk to anybody except to express his wants. Sometimes the man in the mirror spoke—gave orders to the men in his squad, reported to the officers, made things happen that had to happen, as he had always done—but Robert rarely spoke. Speaking was something like eating because it made the edges come out; and if the edges broke through enough and made a big enough hole, his friends would come to visit, and he couldn't have that.

"What is your name?" Robert asked.

"Mañuel Bustos." Manny drew it out, gave it dignity, and raised his head in such a way as to give power to the *tos* on the end of Bustos. Mañuel Bustos. "It is from my father, the name, before he went away and was killed. He was as yourself, a soldier, and went to fight the bandidos in the mountains south of Chihuahua. . . ."

But Robert was not listening because it was not

an answer that mattered. Some of them mattered, and he didn't often listen anyway, but he never listened to answers that didn't matter; and it was clear that the boy was lying because he had to lie. The boy was from the street and if he did not lie he would be dead—he lived where everything was a lie. He had to lie. Robert should not have asked the question, but it was necessary because the boy had been waiting. He should not have asked the name but asked instead what they called him. Then the boy might not have had to lie, but he did not want to ask it now because one question was enough.

Besides, the waiter was starting to bring food. Not the eggs yet but other plates of food; he set them on the table and the boy started to eat. Not like a boy, the eating, but something else Robert had seen. Where was that? Someplace strange he had seen something eat that way—oh yes, it was the monkey. In Saigon. No, wait, not there but in the village in the mountains in the Philippines, up in the Bagio mountains. There had been a monkey on a chain tied to a wire between two trees, and the people who owned the monkey didn't feed it right. Some officer's family that had been, some officer's family, and they thought it was exotic to have the pet monkey tied between the old mango trees in their back yard. But they starved the monkey, and one day they were having a picnic and Robert had been there, had seen it because he was on R-and-R and vacationing in the Bagio mountains. They had a large picnic for other officers, and the monkey broke the wire and came for the picnic table and started to grab and eat and grab and eat. It would look at one thing and grab and eat another, looking always ahead of where it was grabbing to see what it would cram next into its mouth, making up for months and months of being tied to the wire, starving. It stayed ahead of the officers, who were screaming and hitting at it with sticks, and grabbed to eat until it had run through all the food on the table. Then it had turned and gone back, clawing and grabbing and stuffing itself, finally running free up the mango tree.

The boy . . . He ate that way now: looking next at what to clutch in his hand while he stuffed his mouth and chewed and swallowed and grabbed again. He was dirty to grayness, Robert saw, the kind of grayness that didn't wash out—but he was not dirtier than the alleys or the roads or the sides of the buildings.

The waiter brought Robert's eggs, looked distastefully at Manny eating and walked away for more food. Robert cut the eggs small, found the yolks hard, which he liked, and ate them piece by piece, chewing carefully at each piece and swallowing it because it was a duty to eat, only a duty to eat, and food must be chewed correctly. Militarily. The man in the mirror was army property; the body was army property and must be fed correctly, just as the other man, Robert, must be kept close to numbness. It was the correct procedure and he ate the eggs correctly.

The boy watched him now without slowing his own eating, grabbing and stuffing, his hands greasy with food. He had eaten his eggs not with a fork but with his bare hands, and the same for the plate of sausage; his fingers were coated with yolk and grease, and he licked them before starting on the tortillas and beans. There was need for polite conversation, Robert thought. That's what was expected at a meal—polite conversation.

"The monkey did not live long after the picnic," Robert said suddenly. "A snake came and caught him in the tree and swallowed him, but I do not think it was because he ate the picnic food. Justice doesn't often work that well. In true justice the monkey would have eaten the snake if the monkey had enough money."

Manny stared at him but said nothing, kept

eating. He had understood many, most of the words but did not know what a snake was or a picnic or justice or what the words meant the way the sergeant had said them. The sergeant's chest had many medals on it, and Manny thought he must be a very brave man. Perhaps nearly as brave as Pancho Villa.

Robert finished eating. He put his fork down carefully on the plate and leaned back in his chair. The boy was still eating, but Robert had had enough of polite conversation or any kind of conversation. He signaled to the waiter and got the bill and paid for all of the food; he stood and walked out of the café into the morning light without saying anything more.

The waiter looked to be about ready to throw Manny out as well but did not touch him. Manny wiped up the rest of the grease on his plate and the sergeant's plate with a tortilla and ate it, although he had to nearly pack it down his throat into his full stomach. Then he made a package with the paper napkin and wrapped the burritos and two of the sweet rolls and the tube of sweet-meats—all that was left—and scrambled out after the sergeant because there was this he had learned: if such a one came—such a one who would fill a table with food and not complain, who would spend money in that way and ask for nothing—it was like finding gold in the gutter.

If such a one as the sergeant was found, he must not be lost again; but when Manny ran into the street the sergeant was not to be seen. Up, down the street and out onto the tracks there was not a sign of him, not a sign he had ever existed except that Manny's belly was full and his hands were carrying the food.

Gone.

9

*M*anny picked a direction and set off at a trot, down the tracks toward the bullring—the *plaza de toros*. It was a large circular building with doors around the bottom and open on top to let in the sun. Inside there was a huge dirt ring with wooden sides and seats rising in tiers like stone steps. It was the place where they fought the bulls. Manny spent almost no time around the bullring because they had guards so you could not get in without tickets, and even a ticket for the sunny side—hottest and cheapest—cost so much he could never afford it. He had never seen a bullfight. Besides, from what he had heard of bullfights he did not need to see them—a man sticking a bull and killing it was nothing to him, nothing when he had seen men stick men and kill them in the alleys—and it was not a good place to beg. It was all for the turistas, the killing of the bulls, and everything inside the ring was so expensive (cushions for the seats, beer, sun umbrellas, fans) that the turistas did not think kindly of begging children when they came out.

But the ring was a direction to go, and when he rounded the corner of the street that ran past it, he saw he had picked right. The tall sergeant was standing near the main entrance to the ring looking at a poster. Manny had done the same. The poster was full of color and swirls of power, with the bull wrapping around the matador so close he almost touched, following the cape with sharp horns that were white-red and curved barely past the chest of the matador.

"I could tell you much of the fights." Manny stopped alongside the sergeant, panting a bit from running, holding his food in a bundle in his shirt. "I am of course an expert on such things and could help you to understand them if you wish."

Robert gave no sign he heard the boy and indeed was not listening. The colors from the poster were there, were with him now, and the matador, and he thought to see more than there was in the poster but he would have to go to a fight then, to see where the poster came from, and bullfights made no sense because they were not a fight. They were a killing to him and he did not want to sit and see a killing simply to find more color, and yet . . . and yet.

He turned to see the boy, still gray with dirt and with grease on his face from the food, the monkey food he had eaten with his hands, grabbing and shoving it into his mouth. Even as he watched, the boy took another mouthful of food that he had in his hand, his stomach bulging out against the shirt.

"Take care," Robert said slowly, "that a snake does not swallow you so that the chain from your collar hangs out of his mouth."

In some ways Manny was like the Mexican policeman near the bridge when Manny had been held by the sergeant—he had heard and seen most possible things to hear and see in the streets of Juárez. But this tall sergeant was different from any of the others he had seen, different with his hard and soft sides and his evenness. It was as if he was drunk and not drunk at the same time. "I do not understand what you mean. . . ."

But now Robert moved on. He had decided that he had to see the fight, which he already thought of as the killing, because he needed to know more of it, though he didn't want to see it. But it became more complicated because edges were starting to come through definitely now, and that meant he had to find a drink, to curve the edges back. And that meant leaving the ring, going to a liquor store, buying a bottle, coming back to the bullring and getting a ticket, and he did not know when the fights started so he didn't know when he had to be back—and on and on. Life could become so complicated.

"What is it you wish to know?" Manny followed him, trotting at his side as Robert walked around the building looking for a sign that would tell of the fight. "I could find out for you if I knew. . . ."

Before Manny could speak further they came to a small billboard on the wall that gave the information Robert wanted: the fights started at one o'clock and there would be six bulls and three matadors. Robert looked at his watch and found they had three hours still, and he turned to look directly down at Manny for the first time. "We must go to the liquor store and then we must come back and stand and wait until the gates open. It is necessary to go to the fights but we must wait until they open. We will stand near the door to wait. How is that with you?"

This Manny understood and set off to lead Robert to the liquor store, his mind working on the chances of getting money somehow. Surely it must be possible to get American money from this tall sergeant. Not just tickets and food but money.

It was two blocks to the liquor store near the bridge where there were colored banners telling how cheap American whiskey could be here because there was no import duty. But now the edges were coming sharper, the small corners at first but the larger edges following; and if Robert did not use whiskey soon, there would be room in the edges for the friends to come, all the friends, and he could not have that. With Manny trotting at his side, still wondering about how to turn this man into money, true money that he could use to get across the bridge, Robert walked rapidly the last yards to the door and into the liquor store and up to the clerk, who was wearing the same white coat as a doctor in a soap opera.

Robert ordered Cutty Sark Scotch because it

came in a green bottle; he hated the green and hated the bottle and hated Scotch, so it became the perfect whiskey for becoming brain dead, for becoming something he hated but needed to do. Manny stood next to him, watched him order the whiskey, and thought of reaching for the change but knew that would not be wise, so instead he took a bottle of Pepsi. Robert paid for the pop and Manny wished he had taken two of them, but it was too late because Robert was out the door and gone and Manny had to run to catch up. He still had the burrito and one of the candied sweetmeats in his shirt and he worried about losing them.

Never a day like this, he thought, running— not in all of his days a day like this one. To eat all of that food and have food to carry and be off the main street so the larger boys did not see what he had found. Never a day like this, and it was just starting. He must be careful now, very, very careful, not to upset the great sergeant. He must flatter him and work him as he had learned to work soldiers near the bridge when he pretended to be a cripple and begged. He must be right in this, in this handling of the sergeant.

"I lied to you earlier," Manny said when he caught up again to Robert. "When I said that my

father was a brave soldier who died fighting bandidos in the mountains. That was not true."

Robert stopped, turned, and looked down at
Manny, waiting. It was interesting to him that the
boy was admitting to a lie, which was another way
of lying, and he thought to learn from it.

"My father is an animal," Manny continued,
making his face look as sad as he could. "He beats
me if I do not bring him money each day to gamble
on the lottery. He beats me and my mother, who
is already ill and cannot stand much more beating,
and he beats my sisters as well, if I do not come
home with money."

Robert turned and walked toward the bullring
once more. He was back to the normal lie, and
Robert had heard those and done those himself.
He had become so good at them now that he could
tell normal lies to himself, and while he did not
always believe the lies he told himself they often
made him pause to be certain he was lying. The
boy could tell him nothing about lying.

"I have never been to a bullfight," Robert said,
walking. He had broken the seal on the bottle
and pushed the cork back and forth to loosen it,
taking a small sip of the Scotch. It cut on his
tongue and burned a bit because it was not true
Scotch but something bottled in Mexico, but it

did not matter. It had alcohol and that was what mattered. "In fact I have not ever been to a sport held in a ring that was about killing, except once when I was a boy I went to a fair and a man rode a motorcycle inside a ring, going higher and higher until something broke and the boards flew and the man on the motorcycle went through the air and was killed. But I don't think he was supposed to die." He took another drink. "But then I don't know if anything is supposed to die. Do you suppose the bull knows he is supposed to die when he comes into the ring?"

He turned to look briefly at Manny again, stopping. They had returned to the street by the bullring, and Robert found a place by the ticket seller's booth to stand and wait. He would have found a place to sit, but if he sat he would wrinkle his uniform; and while he did not personally care if he had a wrinkled uniform, the man in the mirror would become upset. The sergeant in the mirror was still above all a sergeant in the army and stood straight and tall and did not become wrinkled, and so Robert stood.

And waited.

He waited in a military manner, taking small, neat sips of the whiskey, feeling the edges slowly dulling. Manny stopped next to him, eating his last burrito, cramming it down into his bulging stomach. If the food is in your belly they can not take it from you, he thought. He drank the rest of the Pepsi and licked the sweetness from the hole in the can before throwing it away. He studied the sergeant out of the corner of his eye carefully, gauging the effect of the liquor.

He was clearly one of those who drank until he was not the same, but he did not appear to be a mean one. Some of them, the soldiers who drank until they were not the same, were mean and would watch him—or try to catch him—and do the small things that hurt, twist his arm or ear, cuff him across the head. This sergeant was different, was older and different, and had he been mean he would have hurt Manny the night Manny tried to take his wallet.

He was not mean but he was not like the others in different ways—he did not always seem to hear what Manny said, or perhaps it was that he heard but did not care what Manny said. He would clearly require a different approach if any success was to be had—if Manny was to get money. And there was money here—he had seen it when the sergeant pulled a fold of money out of his wallet to pay for the whiskey.

"They will not sell tickets until the middle of

the day," Manny said, after thinking a moment. "Perhaps in the time to wait you would like something, a pack of cigarettes or some tortillas to have in the ring. They sell beer and food in the ring but it is too expensive. If you were to give me money I could go and bring back something for you."

But again Robert did not answer him. He was studying the poster closely, the poster on the door that showed a massive bull whirling all in color around a matador, following the cape as if he were bolted to the cloth. It reminded Robert of something but he could not think what it was, and he kept trying and nearly had it when Manny stepped forward and ripped the poster from the wall, rolled it in a tube, and handed it to him.

"If you like it, it is yours." Manny made it a sweeping gesture but he had carefully looked both ways before acting. Had the police seen him do it, they would have taken him, or at least beaten him, but they would do nothing if an American had the poster. It was expected of Americans that they take things for themselves. All things. Only rarely were they expected to give them back. Americans took and Americans paid; that was the way of it.

And if the poster could help Manny gain some of the sergeant's money . . .

Robert took the poster with solemn gratitude and tucked it beneath his arm. The whiskey was there now, all of it, and he put the cork back in and held off, not wishing yet to go all the way to brain dead since the edges were dulled, though he did not fully understand why he wanted to be able to watch the bullfight. He said nothing to Manny for a time, the two of them standing in front of the ticket booth—Robert with the poster under his arm, Juárez becoming louder and louder as it filled and took another day. It was getting hot, and Robert let the heat work into his body and mind, did not think, and they waited this way until turistas began to come and the ticket booth opened.

10

*M*anny had never been in the bullring but had heard much of it and wished to stay, wished to stay all day and watch the fights; but it did not work that way because the sergeant changed, grew strange, and would not remain. Manny followed him out.

At first they had taken seats on the shady side of the ring, the most expensive side, and the sergeant paid the extra money for seat cushions— Manny saw again into the wallet, saw the money— and bought a bucket of dark beer to drink with the green bottle of Scotch, and some iced bottles of Pepsi-Cola for Manny. And they sat on the benches waiting for the fights to began.

There were to be six bulls and three matadors, and before each fight the matadors and their assistants walked around the ring in their colored Suits of Light, holding their hats up for the crowd. And even if the audience was mostly turistas, mostly fat American turistas who came only to see what a bullfight was like, even with that Manny could feel much excitement, a tightness.

It was the color, he thought, all the colors and the heat and the sand in the ring and the ring itself, to sit high in this manner and look down on the ring where the fight would soon be—all of that was an excitement, a sight to make the breath stop.

Manny did not notice what was happening to Robert sitting next to him. Robert was looking down into the ring, and the excitement had gone into him as well—the noise of the brass band playing the march before the fights began, the heat, the yelling crowd—but in the dust and noise and color Robert moved off inside himself, moved off just a little distance and the sergeant in the mirror came instead.

His nostrils grew tight and he looked on this

with a flatness, a waiting of flat gray iron eyes; his back was rigid; and there was not thought, only the waiting for blood, for the fight, as the man in the mirror had waited so many times before—flat wait. A wait with everything ready. Fight wait. Death wait.

Now the ring cleared of all men and there was a change in the music, a heralding of horns, and large doors at one end opened. A bull, a black bull with enormous shoulders and a curved, thick neck, curling horns glistening gray black, thundered into the ring, wheeled with a toss, and looked for something to attack.

Manny held his breath at sight of the bull. He was all things strong, all powerful, as he stood looking around the ring, throwing dirt back with small kicks on his front feet. And Robert stiffened beside him now, stiffened and whispered.

"This is all to mean something," he said, his voice tight and even. "This in the ring now is all to mean something, but it doesn't . . . it means nothing. It is for nothing."

The fight progressed rapidly. Even though he hadn't seen one, Manny knew the stages of a fight. First the picador came, a heavy man on a horse, using a short lance with a knife tip to cut down into the bull's shoulder so his head would drop—to cut and tear the shoulder. And when this was done, with the bull goring the horse and lifting him, ramming a horn into his stomach so the horse would later die, making the turistas cheer and yell "Olé!" again and again as the smell from the blood of the horse and the fresh pumping blood of the bull's torn shoulders rose up from the ring—when this was done, Robert was completely changed, and he stood, stood alone, watching only the bull.

"For nothing," he said again. And now Manny looked up at him, realizing the change, and at first he could not understand who the sergeant was talking to, could not decide until he saw the sergeant's eyes, going out to the bull, and knew that he was speaking only to the bull. His voice was soft, almost gentle, explaining a thing he knew well. "All of this is to mean something and it's for nothing. Only a game."

And so he remained for the whole fight. The sergeant stood watching the bull, understanding the bull in softness while they wheeled about him again and again with the capes and stuck the colored, barbed sticks—the bandilerros—in his shoulders to keep the head still further down, taking the bull not into beauty but only into spinning ugliness and blood-stink, slaughtering it in the sun and dirt. Finally, the matador drove the killing sword down through the bull's shoulders and into its chest; finally, it coughed bright blood and sank to its knees and died, stinking in the sun and blood and dirt.

"A game," the sergeant whispered when it was done, the turistas screaming and clapping. "All for nothing—always all for nothing. I should not have come to this." And he wheeled and walked through the crowd, parting them like a hot wind, through the crowd and out into the street and back to the Club Congo Tiki—where the bouncer stopped the following Manny and where Robert walked through the mouth of the native and found his corner and ordered the drinks to put his brain away again. And that was the second meeting.

THE
THIRD
MEETING
AND
AFTER

11

It was not hard for Manny to remember when he began to think of things other than money with the tall sergeant. It was just after the third meeting. And it had come as a surprise.

He had not seen the sergeant for a week, and in that week he had gone back to the street, back to begging and working at the bridge with the cardboard cones for the small money, but it had been bad for him. Maria fed him when she could at the Two-by-Four, but the owner did not want him hanging around the back door. And there was no other food to be had except for bits at the market, and many other boys worked the market. Under the bridge he was constantly beaten and any money he had won was taken from him so that if he caught a coin he had to run at once, and with speed, to keep the money and his skin.

Not good. None of it good. No money to cross, and not a way to live in Juárez. Twice he had seen the men who had nearly taken him the night on the river, but they did not see him and he moved into the alleys away from them. His life was getting closer, tighter and leaner when he met the sergeant the third time.

It was once more in the alley behind the Congo Tiki in the early morning. Manny had moved his sleeping from the back of the church to a warm doorway in the rear of the dentist's shop because the man had a smelter for melting down old dental plates and the smelter left heat for hours in the door opening. The nights were starting to get cool as the summer faded, and the heat allowed him to sleep more comfortably. His new bed was down the alley from the Congo Tiki, and as he was coming back from begging by the bridge—with nothing for his night's work—he looked up to see the sergeant step out of the doorway to lean against the wall and be sick.

Manny stepped back in the shadow and watched silently. He had seen many soldiers sick, but not in this way, not in a planned way, and he wondered how the sergeant could control himself so well and yet drink so much. The last time Manny had seen him, at the bullfight, he had had whiskey and beer all day and had not gotten to the point of weaving. But he was drunk now, and the rule with drunk soldiers, even when you knew them, was to work for money—it was the best time to get money.

"Hola, sergeant." Manny stepped out of the shadow and moved closer. "How have you been?"

Robert cleaned himself and looked down at the boy, working to remember, then smiled. "The monkey—I wondered what had happened to you. I thought perhaps the snake had swallowed you."

Manny knew nothing of monkeys or snakes but he shrugged. "I looked for you, after the bullfight, and for many nights here but you did not come out."

Robert said nothing, thinking now of the fight, remembering the afternoon and the bull, how the bull had gone down slowly, and he thought how when he had gone back to the barracks he had not been able to stop thinking about the bull for nearly a week. And the bull had mixed with the other friends, and he had fought to keep him away—down that way with his muzzle bleeding into the dirt in his mind, staggering down like some of the others. He had stayed in his room after work for that week, sitting and drinking alone until he had controlled the friends and the bull.

"I must walk to the bridge now. . . ." He set off in the cool morning dark and Manny followed at a trot.

"I have been busy myself," Manny said. "My father beat me and made me work twice as hard for money. I have whip marks on my back." It was a good lie in that a part of it was at least slightly true. He had marks on his back, and he ran ahead to a streetlight and pulled his shirt up to show them. And it only mattered a little that they were from boys hitting him with their money sticks under the bridge and not a father—they were still good marks—but Robert did not stop. Though Manny worked hard at the story and told of the beatings in detail and how his father was in a rage, it did not help.

Finally, at the bridge where Manny could not go, Robert stopped and turned and handed Manny a five-dollar bill. It was so sudden, so abrupt that he almost did not grab it, hesitated for half a beat before he snatched at the money and jammed it into his pocket. Then he looked up at the sergeant's face and did not see the sergeant, the hard man, but something softer for a moment. "Thank you. . . ."

For part of a second the softness stayed. Then it was gone. "It was what you wanted. It was always what you wanted."

Robert turned then and walked across the bridge and left Manny standing there, the money in his pocket, watching after him, and for a moment, for half a breath Manny did not think of money. He thought instead of the softness and thought that it was the same softness the tall one had in his eyes when he spoke down to the bull as they hacked him to death.

Then he turned and ran for the alley. He would have to hide with the money before some of the large ones smelled it. Money always smelled, and somehow the smell went out to the larger boys and they knew when he had it; and the plan did not come to him until he was curled in the doorway and pulling a piece of cardboard over his shoulders.

He had five dollars in his pocket. Five dollars of American money and that would be enough to cross. To cross. Except that if he saw the sergeant the next night and the next perhaps it was so that the tall man would have more money, and that thought brought the plan. What if he were to tell the sergeant the truth?

Sleep was near now, or not sleep so much as the doze in and out that made for sleep in the alleys. What if he told the sergeant all of the truth about what he wanted to do and asked the sergeant for help, and how would that be? He had never told anyone the truth before.

How would that be?

12

The next night Robert looked down on the
boy in the alley, the dark alley, and thought how
this new thing was—how it was that the boy was
not lying, that the boy had to lie to live and yet
had stopped lying and was telling Robert the truth.
When even to think the truth was dangerous, was
to show weakness in the streets or in a war—as
Robert knew—the boy was telling the truth.

"I do not know of my father," Manny said. "Or
my mother. I know nothing but being young with
the nuns and then the streets and how it is to live

in the streets. I have no sisters, no mother, nothing. I have only what I am."

What is this, Robert thought—he had heard all this before. No. Not in this way. But what was coming—that part he had heard. Oh God, he had heard that part that was coming when they asked for help and expected him to be able to help. Again and again he had heard that part. In the green places when they had been hurt, hurt to death, and asked him for help leaning against the earth; with the dry spit in their voices and the short panting of their breath they had asked for help and there was nothing he could do for them then and he could see nothing he could do for this boy now.

"I cannot live in the streets much longer. I am too small." Manny shrugged. "It is as Maria said— I am too small. Soon the hawks will get me and they will sell me as they do."

Soon, Robert thought—soon the hawks will get us all and we will never be the same again.

Manny looked away, down the alley. All of this was true and he had never told the truth as it was, as it really was, and he felt strange. Years of lying— and how it was as if a dam burst and he wanted to tell all things as they truly were, tell them to an American sergeant who had just been sick against the back wall of a drinking place in an alley in Juárez. Such a man to ask for help. "I do not have much longer. . . ." He finished lamely.

And so, Robert thought—he wants me to ask. I cannot help and he thinks I can and he wants me to ask. They all wanted me to ask. All of those leaning against the earth wanted me to ask. "What is it you want me to do?"

Manny looked up at his face. The question had been clear, the voice even, not drunk-sounding. "It is said that on the other side, if you get across you can get a green card so that you can be in the open, and there are places for children to live where they are fed and have a roof. Is this so?"

And golden highways, Robert thought, and all the dreams come true and nobody is ever sad again. He nodded.

"And it is further said that if somebody helps you, somebody who is a Norte Americano helps you, that it is not impossible for all that to happen. Is that so?"

Two cars, Robert thought. Three meals a day and two cars and a big house with a swimming pool and a fenced yard and a garage door that opens automatically and a large-screen color television and sweepstake lottery tickets and football games and cheerleaders and bank accounts

and stock brokers and green lawns and a day at
the office and coming home from work and toys
that clutter a room and tables heavy with food
and schoolyards crowded with children and the
Superbowl and fancy clothes and expensive hair
and shoes—God, shoes that cost a fortune—and
more, and more, and always more—a diet bread
now made of wood fiber that has no food value
so people can continue to overeat without getting
fat. Robert looking at Manny's face. "There are
many who spend more on one car, one time, than
you can earn here in your entire life."

Manny did not hear it. He was in the truth now,
seeing what a thing it was, the truth. "But if there
is help is it not possible to get the green card and
live in such a place where there is food and a roof?
Is that not possible? Is not all of this possible if
you get across?"

And always more, Robert thought. And always
more. He nodded again. "All things are possible
if you get across; that is what I hear."

"Would you help me?"

There it is, Robert thought. There it all is just
as they always asked in the jungle places with the
spit in their voices when there was nothing I could
do for them, when they leaned against the earth

and died and asked, it was the same way—will you help me?

But now his head moved, without his thinking of it or meaning it to, alone his head moved and nodded once more, and his lips opened and he said: "Yes. I will help you." And to his complete amazement he meant it, meant that he would help when he had long ago decided he could help no other person in the world just as he could no longer help himself except by drinking to keep the friends away. "I will help you."

He thought it and meant it and turned to walk to the bridge, thinking he would take a pass the next day and see the legal officer about papers and helping small Mexican children, thinking he would do all these things before he used the whiskey for the day to stop the edges, thinking he would do all these things—when he sensed Manny stop beside him, and Robert looked up to see four men standing across the alley.

"See," one of them said softly, "it is the small red-haired one and his man."

I know this, Robert thought. I know how this will be. A shouldering happened in his mind, a nudge of something pushing sideways, and he stopped thinking; and the man in the mirror came in, came in to wait in the flat gray place he always waited.

Next to him Manny felt the sergeant tense, felt his body change and grow slightly, felt him coil, but could see nothing in the near darkness. He was afraid. There was not a way out of the alley except through them and there were four of them and they would get him, would take him and sell him.

"It is time for you to leave, American soldier," the same man said quietly. "We have work with the small one, not with you."

Robert did not move, still said nothing. They did not want talk. They never wanted talk, and he knew all of how this worked now. The man in the mirror was there, above all things a sergeant, above all things a soldier, and he knew this: they did not want talk. They wanted only the other thing, the thing he had done so often and knew all about and was so good at doing.

The ending of it.

He was good at that and they did not understand; they thought that because there were four of them they did not have to have fear, but he knew this, knew what would come.

And it did.

One of them, the same one who had spoken,

pulled something out of his shirt and there was a quick sound, a metal sound, and a knife blade caught the light from the end of the alley. Two others brought knives out then and moved to the side, and the fourth one brought out a piece of chain; and still Robert did not move, still he stood, his arms at his sides, hands slightly forward, feet apart and planted evenly and firmly on the alley concrete, face to the front.

He does not have fear, Manny thought, glancing up at him. How could he not have fear? In his chest Manny's heart was a roar, filling his ears, and he thought only of running; but there was not a place to run and he could not fight, could not do anything to hurt the stealers of boys. They had knives, silver blades in the dark, and he could do nothing to them and was afraid of dying, but the sergeant had no fear.

"It is time for you to leave," the man with the knife said again. "Go home, gringo. . . ."

"I'll stay."

The man nodded. "I thought you would. Still, there are four of us. Does that not bother you?"

Robert said nothing. The talk was over now; now it was time for the end. Manny saw his arms come up slightly, the hands forming in semi-fists, saw the sergeant's back roll with a tightening, saw the hand swing and the rhythm of something come into him; and when he looked up at the sergeant's face it had changed, was hard and lined, edged and cutting, wild-looking, even and wild.

The four men were apart now and moved at him from the front and sides. When they were close, three feet away, one of them feinted with a knife. They were like the street dogs, one to jump in and the next to hit, they worked the same way. The first one feinted and another moved in, slashing with the knife and moving back, and blood came on the sergeant's arm—on his right arm in a line down from the shoulder—but before the blood and before the man could move back there was a movement in the sergeant's hands, a floating out of the hands and a cracking sound, and the man who had faked first lay on the ground with his head back in a strange manner, his feet twitching.

For a second, two seconds, nothing happened. All Manny could hear was the breathing of the men and his own heart and the dripping of something he realized was the sergeant's blood from the cut on his arm, dripping to the pavement. The man on the ground was dead, he knew that— knew the terrible thing the sergeant could do.

Two seconds, three more, still and silent; then all three came for him, came for the sergeant, and

Manny moved into a doorway and saw them, saw the cutting of the knives as they licked at the sergeant. And it was like the bullfight for Manny, the hacking of the bull, except that the sergeant, the tall one, took a terrible toll. They flicked and cut and stabbed and slashed, and always his hands moved, and when they moved they broke something, crippled something, and all in silence. All in silent seconds it was done, and the sergeant was on his knees, soaked in blood, holding his stomach with one hand and his neck with another, settling lower and lower on his heels, on his legs until he was sitting back, almost at rest, except that it was a rest that would not, could not end.

Around him the four men lay, not moving, and Manny heard a sharp hiss, an explosive hiss that was his breath. He'd been holding it, and now he jumped forward.

"Madre de Dios," he whispered. "Mother of God—I have never seen such a thing. . . ."

Robert looked at him, but the eyes were changing now, were not those of the man in the mirror, but the other one, the one from the bullfight; and even as he looked at Manny the eyes were clouding, were graying. Manny reached for him, to help him down, but the sergeant shook the hand away. He removed the hand from his stomach and reached for his back pocket, dug at something and pulled at it until his bloody hand held it up to Manny.

It was the wallet.

"No," Manny said. "Not in this way. No."

"Take it," Robert said now. "Take it and run and cross and get the green card and live there. It is what you want. What I want you to have. Take it and run before there are police here, little monkey, and do not let the snake . . ."

And there would have been more—more was in his mind to say to Manny, so much more was there to say to Manny but it could not get through the pain now, the wounds—and the tall one's eyes became the same as the bull's eyes, the same to Manny.

Robert felt the edges, and the friends started to come through, to meet him, to be with him; and Robert did not fear them now but knew what they wanted, what they had always wanted. He smiled at them and greeted them and could not see Manny any longer, could see nothing as he settled slowly back, then forward and down, could not see Manny cry and pull at him and, finally, when there was nothing else to do and the police were coming, Robert could not see Manny run with the wallet, run in the dark, run for the river and the crossing.

F
PAU
Pausen, Gary.
The crossing

F
PAU
Pausen, Gary.
The crossing

DATE DUE
